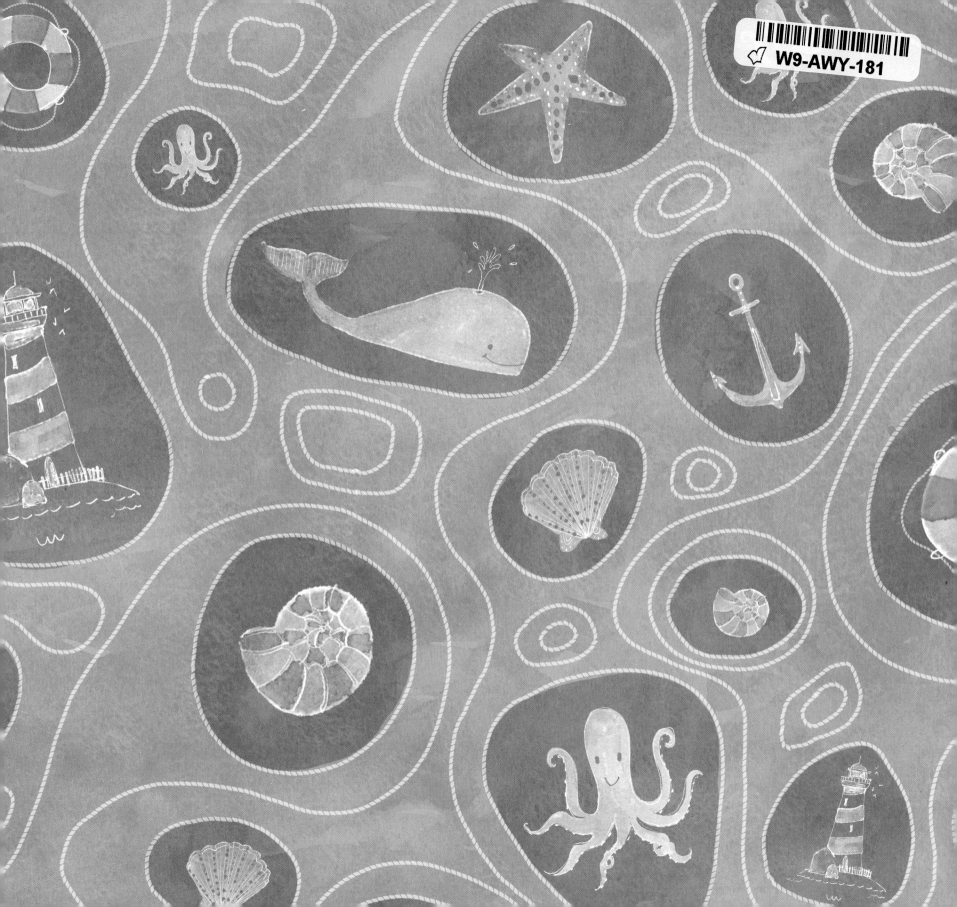

For Canaan, Wyatt, Sebastian, and Annabelle —J.C.

For my son, Emerson —L.W.

Text copyright © 2017 by Julie Case
Jacket art and interior illustrations copyright © 2017 by Lee White

All rights reserved. Published in the United States by Schwartz & Wade Books, an imprint of
Random House Children's Books, a division of Penguin Random House LLC, New York.
Schwartz & Wade Books and the colophon are trademarks of Penguin Random House LLC.

Visit us on the Web! randomhousekids.com
Educators and librarians, for a variety of teaching tools, visit us at RHTeachersLibrarians.com

Library of Congress Cataloging-in-Publication Data
Names: Case, Julie, author. | White, Lee, illustrator.
Title: Emma and the whale / Julie Case, Lee White.
Description: First edition. | New York : Schwartz & Wade Books, [2017] | Summary: Emma,
a young girl with an affinity for the ocean, finds a baby whale beached on the shore and tries to save her.
Identifiers: LCCN 2016000768 | ISBN 978-0-553-53847-2 (hc) | ISBN 978-0-553-53848-9 (glb) | ISBN 978-0-553-53849-6 (ebook)
Subjects: | CYAC: Ocean—Fiction. | Beaches—Fiction. | Whales—Fiction. | Wildlife rescue—Fiction.
Classification: LCC PZ7.1.C435 Em 2017 | DDC [E]—dc23

The text of this book is set in P22 Sherwood.
The illustrations were rendered in watercolor and mixed media and manipulated digitally.
Book design by Rachael Cole

MANUFACTURED IN CHINA
2 4 6 8 10 9 7 5 3 1
First Edition

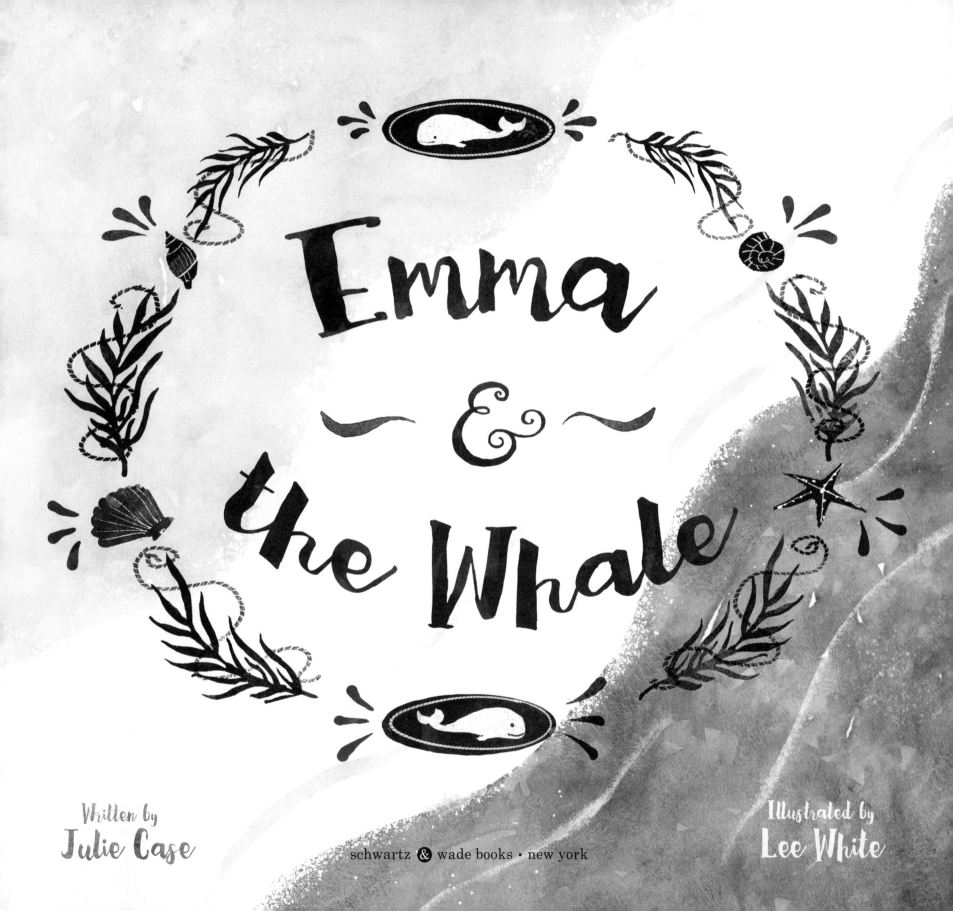

Emma & the Whale

Written by
Julie Case

Illustrated by
Lee White

schwartz & wade books · new york

The old house where Emma lived had crooked walls and slanting floors, but Emma didn't mind. It was close to the ocean, and that was her favorite place to be.

After school, Emma always took her dog, Nemo, to play at the beach. They combed the shore for shells and stones and sea glass. At low tide, that's when they found the best treasures.

Sometimes Emma saw
whales in the water.

Sometimes she saw dolphins,

and once a loggerhead turtle. She liked to
picture an ocean teeming with life, with no
balloons or bottles spit to shore.

THE WHALES!

Emma often imagined traveling back to olden times,
when whalers had lived in her seaside hamlet. She would
shout at the captains, "Please don't hurt the whales!"
And they would listen.

One foggy day, Emma grabbed a small bucket because the tide was low and her green jacket because she thought it might rain. She and Nemo headed down Beach Lane toward the ocean. Emma felt droplets on her cheeks. She smelled the salty air. The sea and the sky swirled together as she skipped past the misty dunes to the shoreline.

Emma and Nemo frolicked in the surf. They followed the tide line. They sank their toes in the sand. The drizzle began softly, but Emma had her cozy wool sweater and her jacket to keep her warm. *We're having minestrone soup and rosemary bread for dinner,* she thought. *I'll turn around soon.*

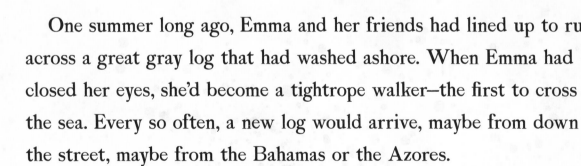

One summer long ago, Emma and her friends had lined up to run across a great gray log that had washed ashore. When Emma had closed her eyes, she'd become a tightrope walker—the first to cross the sea. Every so often, a new log would arrive, maybe from down the street, maybe from the Bahamas or the Azores.

Nemo started barking. *That's so unlike him,* thought
Emma. She followed Nemo's stare down the beach.
What is that? she wondered. *I think it's a drift log.*

Then she realized. *It's not a log.*

It's a **whale!**

Emma ran closer. "I'm not going to hurt you,"
she whispered, kneeling down.

The whale stretched across the sand—a dark body, tail, flippers,
and pectoral fins. Emma looked at its big black eye. The wide-eyed
whale stared back. "You must be a baby. I'm a friend. I will help you."

Thank you. The whale's voice sounded in her head.

"Did you just speak to me?"

I did, Emma felt the whale reply.

Bigger raindrops fell, and Emma put her hand on the whale's back. She felt its breaths. She saw its blowhole. Emma felt the suffering in that big body. She couldn't say how, but she knew the whale was a girl, like her. "I have to get you back to the water," Emma said.

Emma and the whale watched as waves
arrived on shore, uncurled, and swept back to
sea. *The ocean never stops,* Emma marveled.

The tide was coming in. It reached a flipper. "The water's rising," she said. "Soon you can swim home."

I'm scared!

"Don't be," Emma replied. "Think of your pod, and your family. Picture yourself swimming free."

She touched the little whale. "It's time."
The whale was even heavier than
she looked.

Emma pushed hard and tumbled onto her.
"I'm sorry!" Emma's eyes welled with tears.

She took a deep breath and tried again. *I can do this.*

As the waves unrolled, Emma pushed and pushed and pushed. The whale began to wriggle.

The surf swirled around them. The water got deeper, and the ocean did the work.

A few more pushes, and the whale slipped past
Emma and ducked under a wave.

She was beyond the break, over the sandbar,
and out to sea.

Emma saw the whale look back. A bit beyond,
another whale hovered.

That must be her mother. Emma stood stunned,
breathless and sopping wet.

She watched the whales swim off together.
"Goodbye!" she called.

Goodbye, goodbye,
goodbye, the whale's song rang.

The whales disappeared into the fog. Emma remained in the shallowest water. Nemo lingered on the sand. "Nemo!" Emma shouted, and ran to her dog. She hugged him tightly, and they started for home.

That night, sleep came easily, and Emma dreamed of the whale.
Her legs wrapped around the whale's big back. They sailed through
turquoise waters, beside pink sand beaches. Emma gripped the
whale's back with her knees. Her hair was loose. Her arms reached
out, and she was laughing.

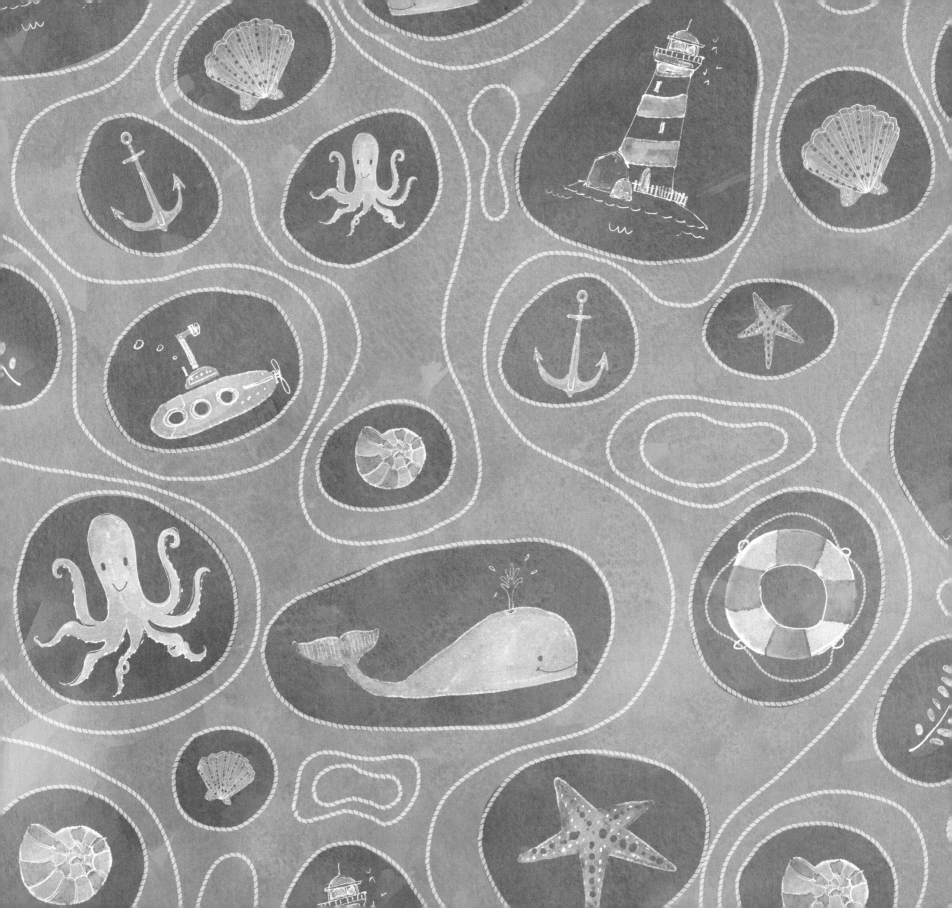